LET'S COLOUR IRELAND!

With me —
Deirdre the Dolphin!

WRITTEN AND ILLUSTRATED BY
ALAN NOLAN

THE O'BRIEN PRESS
DUBLIN

NEWGRANGE

Newgrange, a gigantic passage tomb in County Meath, is older than both Stonehenge and the Egyptian pyramids. The Neolithic people who built it decorated the rocks with beautiful patterns, spirals and triskelles. On 21 December every year, light from the rising sun enters the tomb's long passage, lighting up the inner chamber and revealing the carvings in the stones.

WHERE IN IRELAND?

County Meath

OTA WILDLIFE PARK

Fota Wildlife Park is on Fota Island in Cork Harbour. Ireland's only wildlife park opened its gates in 1983 and is home to over 70 species of exotic wildlife, from antelope to zebras. It's also home to a few cheeky monkeys!

County Cork

THE ROCK OF CASHEL

The Rock of Cashel dates from the 10th century and was once the home of the kings of Munster. Some people say when Saint Patrick, Ireland's patron saint, was fighting with the Devil on a mountain in north Tipperary, the Devil threw a huge rock which missed the saint completely and landed in the town of Cashel. The mountain they were fighting on is called the Devil's Bit.

WHERE IN IRELAND?

County Tipperary

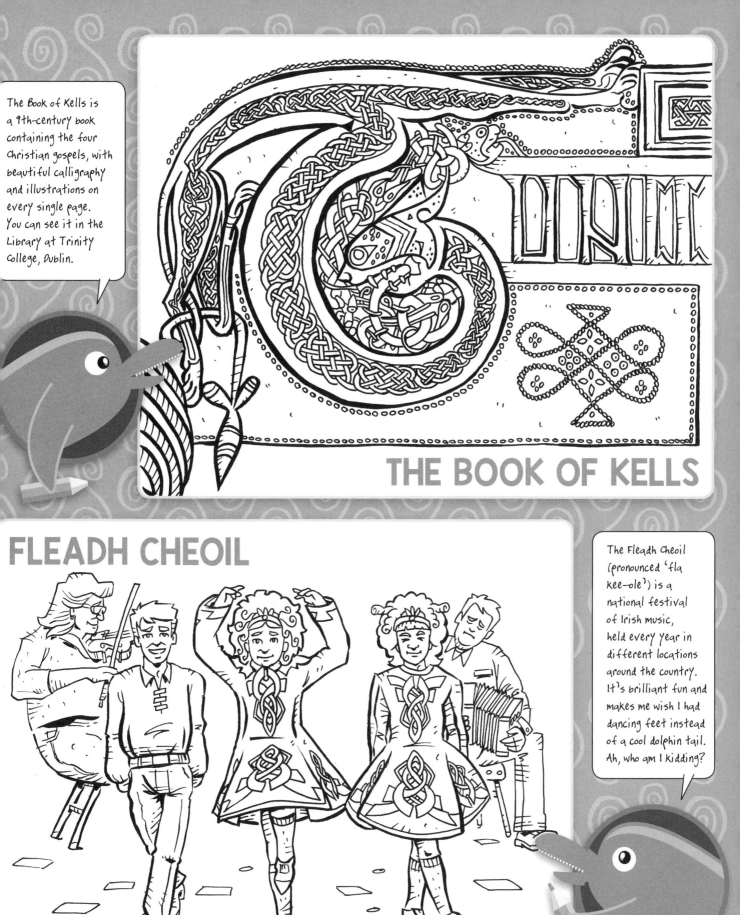

The Book of Kells is a 9th-century book containing the four Christian gospels, with beautiful calligraphy and illustrations on every single page. You can see it in the Library at Trinity College, Dublin.

THE BOOK OF KELLS

FLEADH CHEOIL

The Fleadh Cheoil (pronounced 'fla kee-ole') is a national festival of Irish music, held every year in different locations around the country. It's brilliant fun and makes me wish I had dancing feet instead of a cool dolphin tail. Ah, who am I kidding?

THE TITANIC

The RMS Titanic was built in the world-famous Harland and Wolff shipyards in Belfast and, when it was completed in 1912, it was the largest ship in the world. Three thousand workers spent two years building the ship, and twenty horses were needed to transport its massive anchor. But, on its maiden voyage on 14 April 1912, the Titanic hit an iceberg and sank in the early hours of the next morning.

TITANIC

TITANIC COMPLETED

WHERE IN IRELAND?

Belfast City

PANISH ARCH

County Galway

THE DARK HEDGES

The Dark Hedges is an atmospheric avenue of beech trees on the Bregagh Road in County Antrim. They are said to be haunted by the Grey Lady, the ghostly daughter of the wealthy landowner who originally planted the trees.

The Dark Hedges has been used as a location in the TV series 'Game of Thrones', so be thankful it's only a ghost and not a dragon that can sometimes be seen flitting from tree to tree!

WHERE IN IRELAND?

County Antrim

KELLIG MICHAEL

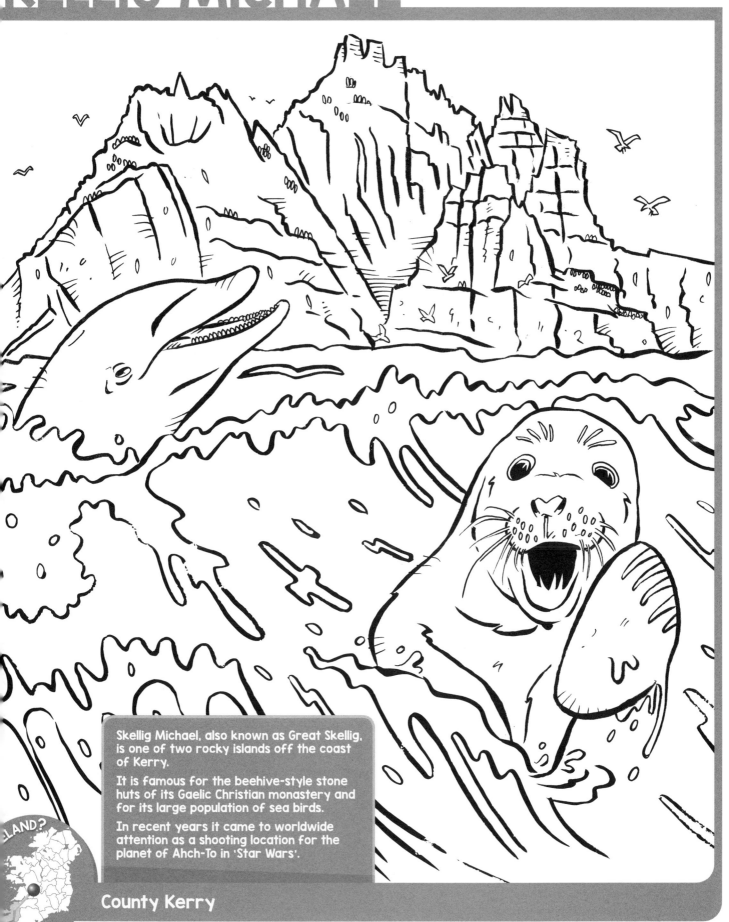

Skellig Michael, also known as Great Skellig, is one of two rocky islands off the coast of Kerry.

It is famous for the beehive-style stone huts of its Gaelic Christian monastery and for its large population of sea birds.

In recent years it came to worldwide attention as a shooting location for the planet of Ahch-To in 'Star Wars'.

County Kerry

MALIN HEAD

Malin head, on the Inishowen Peninsula in County Donegal, is the most northerly point on the island of Ireland. The very top tip of it is called Banba's Crown, after one of the mythical queens of Ireland. From above, you can see the word 'EIRE', spelled out using stones. During the Second World War, this signalled to warplanes that they were flying over neutral territory!

WHERE IN IRELAND?

County Donegal

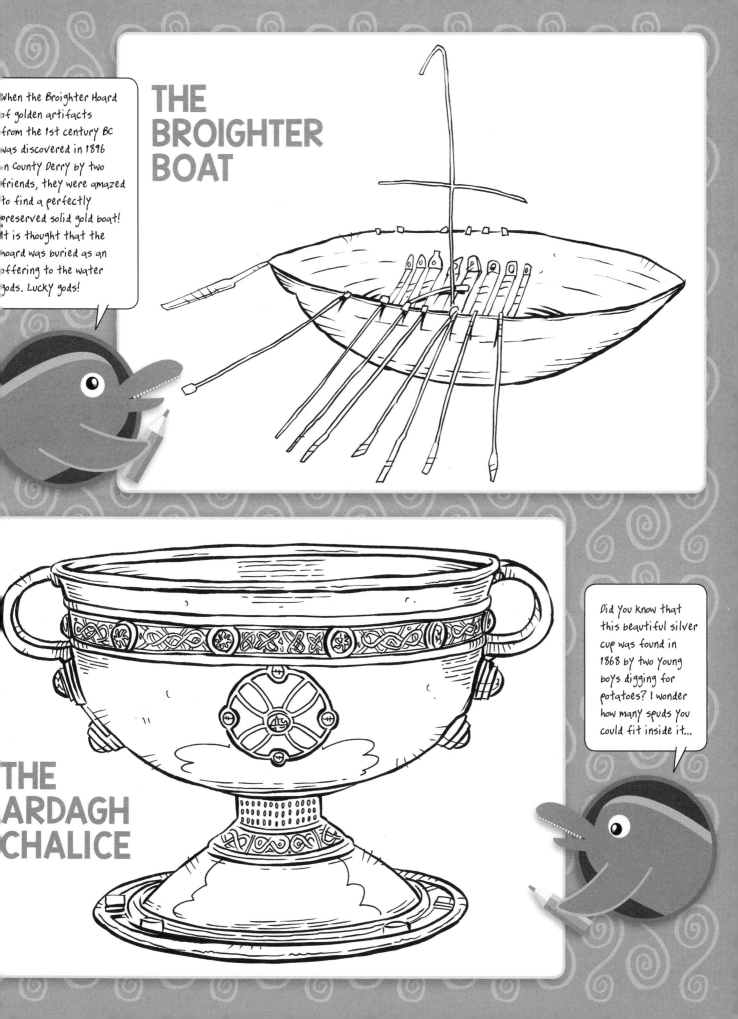

THE BROIGHTER BOAT

When the Broighter Hoard of golden artifacts from the 1st century BC was discovered in 1896 in County Derry by two friends, they were amazed to find a perfectly preserved solid gold boat! It is thought that the hoard was buried as an offering to the water gods. Lucky gods!

THE ARDAGH CHALICE

Did you know that this beautiful silver cup was found in 1868 by two young boys digging for potatoes? I wonder how many spuds you could fit inside it...

KILKENNY CASTLE

Work on building Kilkenny Castle was begun by Richard de Clare, otherwise known as Strongbow, in the 12th century. The Butler family bought the castle in 1391 and lived there until it fell into disrepair. The family sold the castle in the mid-20th century for £50! It is now fully restored and is one of the most popular tourist sites in Ireland.

County Kilkenny

OSSES POINT

Rosses Point is situated at the entrance to Sligo Harbour from Sligo Bay and is surrounded by beaches which are perfect for swimming and surfing. The impressive 'Waiting on Shore' monument near the Rosses Point lifeboat station is dedicated to seafarers: a woman holds her arms out to sea, waiting her loved ones to return.

County Sligo

THE BOTANIC GARDENS

The Botanic Gardens in Glasnevin is home to 20,000 living plants and millions of dried plant specimens from all over the world.

The British Queen Victoria and her husband Prince Albert visited the gardens in 1849, but they didn't have to wait in line like normal tourists - they were lucky enough to be given a private tour!

WHERE IN IRELAND?

County Dublin

FUNGIE

Dingle Bay is home to my old pal, Fungie, Ireland's most famous dolphin. Named by the fishermen who see him each morning as he accompanies their boats out to sea, this playful, mischievous bottlenose weighs in at around 250kg and is almost four metres in length!

THATCHED COTTAGE

Thatched cottages can be seen all over Ireland. These little houses are lovely and cosy, with a huge stone fireplace right in the centre. The roofs are often insulated with turf and the outsides covered in a thatch of straw, heather or rushes. The thatched roofs are so warm that sometimes mice and pine martins make their home inside!

SEMPLE STADIUM

Located in Thurles, County Tipperary, Semple Stadium is the home of women's camogie, men's hurling and Gaelic football for Tipperary GAA, as well as the Munster Hurling Final. This fine 53,000-seat stadium is second only in size to Dublin's Croke Park. The fast-moving team game of camogie was created by two women, Máire Ní Chinnéide and Cáit Ní Dhonnchadha, in 1903.

WHERE IN IRELAND?

County Tipperary

MONDELLO RACETRACK

Mondello Park, located in Caragh, County Kildare, is Ireland's only motor sport venue. It has held rounds of the British Touring Car Championships and the British Superbike Championships, as well as the British Formula 3 Championships. This tricky track features as a racetrack in several videogames.

County Kildare

GLENDALOUGH

The Irish name for Glendalough means 'valley of two lakes' and it is situated in the beautiful Wicklow Mountains National Park. Glendalough is famous for its early medieval monastery, complete with a round tower, which was founded by Saint Kevin. The monks here were renowned for their hospitality.

WHERE IN IRELAND?

County Wicklow

The walled city of Derry, also called Londonderry, lies on the west bank of the River Foyle in County Derry and is one of the best walled cities in Europe.

It is the fourth largest city in Ireland and the only one with its medieval walls completely intact! The walls are 1,600 metres in length and vary in width from 3.7 to 10.7 metres.

Derry's walls have never been breached by an invading force, withstanding many sieges since they were built in 1619.

Derry City

HOOK LIGHTHOUSE

Hook Lighthouse, on Hook Head in County Wexford, is the second oldest operating lighthouse in the world, after the Tower of Hercules in Spain. Standing four stories high and with walls up to 4 metres thick, this medieval tower was built in the 13th century to guide boats bound for the port of New Ross through the dangerous fogs and away from Hook Head's treacherous rocks.

WHERE IN IRELAND?

County Wexford

BLARNEY CASTLE

The medieval keep of Blarney Castle was built in the 15th century. It is home to the Blarney Stone, or 'the Stone of Eloquence'.

It is thought that kissing the Blarney Stone, which is located high up in the castle wall, will give a person the 'gift of the gab'!

The beautiful gardens surrounding the keep are home to several natural rock formations such as the Druid's Circle, the Witch's Cave and the Wishing Steps.

I KISSED THE BLARNEY STONE!

County Cork

CONNEMARA PONIES

Connemara is a large region stretching from County Galway to County Mayo, and includes much of the Irish-speaking Gaeltacht area. It is also home to the sturdy Connemara pony, said to be either a mix of native Irish horses and Scandinavian horses brought to Ireland by Vikings, or Andalusian horses, from shipwrecks during the Spanish Armada.

WHERE IN IRELAND?

County Galway

CLONMACNOISE

The early Christian monastery of Clonmacnoise was founded in 544 AD by Saint Ciarán, and is famous for the beautiful Clonmacnoise Crozier – a bishop's ornamental staff – and three imposing high crosses.

County Offaly

THE PHOENIX PARK

The Phoenix Park in Dublin City is 1,750 acres in size, making it one of the biggest urban parks in Europe! It's home to Dublin Zoo and Áras an Uachtaráin, where the President of Ireland lives. It's also home to a herd of wild fallow deer. Ah, there's one now — hello, dear!

ÁRAS AN UACHTARÁIN

Áras an Uachtaráin was built in 1751 and is the home and workplace of the President of Ireland. Many famous people such as Nelson Mandela, Pope John Paul II and Queen Elizabeth II have visited the house, and you can too — there are guided tours every Saturday!

EGINALD'S TOWER

Reginald's Tower is situated on the city quay in Waterford. Its name is an Anglicised form of the Old Norse Røgnvaldr, a name shared by many of the Viking rulers of the city. Seventeen towers guarded the city in medieval times. Six of those towers are still standing today!

County Waterford

THE RIVER SHANNON

The Shannon is the longest river in Ireland and runs through the provinces of Connacht, Leinster and Munster. The river is named after the Celtic goddess Sionna, pronounced 'shuna', and was first mapped in the first century AD by the Graeco-Egyptian geographer, Claudius Ptolemy. Today, the Shannon and its many lakes are visited by lots of people on boating holidays who often stop at some of the scenic towns along the river, such as Carrick-on-Shannon in County Leitrim.

WHERE IN IRELAND?

Counties Cavan, Leitrim, Roscommon, Longford, Offaly, Westmeath, Galway, Clare, Tipperary, Limerick and Kerry

ARAN ISLANDS

The currach, a boat traditionally made with a wooden frame over which animal skins or hides are stretched, has been used in the Aran Islands and in the seas off the west coast of Ireland since Neolithic times. Nowadays the frames are covered with tarred canvas, and the boats are used to transport goods and livestock from the mainland to the islands.

The Aran Islands have a rich and unique culture of literature, textiles and language that has survived into modern times.

County Galway

POULNABRONE DOLMEN

The Poulnabrone (pronounced 'pole na brone') Dolmen is a Neolithic portal tomb in the rocky Burren in County Clare, near the village of Ballyvaughan. When it was excavated in the 1980s, thirty-three human skeletons were discovered under its massive stones, along with a polished stone axe, a bone pendant, pottery, quartz crystals and weapons – everything a Neolithic warrior would need in the afterlife!

WHERE IN IRELAND?

County Clare

The Treaty Stone stands beside the river Shannon facing the Norman King John's Castle in Limerick City. The story goes that the Treaty of Limerick, which ended the 1688-1691 Williamite War between the Jacobites and the forces of William of Orange, was signed on this humble limestone block.

THE TREATY OF LIMERICK
SIGNED
AD 1693

County Limerick

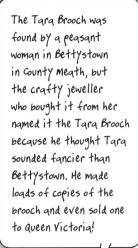

The Tara Brooch was found by a peasant woman in Bettystown in County Meath, but the crafty jeweller who bought it from her named it the Tara Brooch because he thought Tara sounded fancier than Bettystown. He made loads of copies of the brooch and even sold one to Queen Victoria!

THE TARA BROOCH

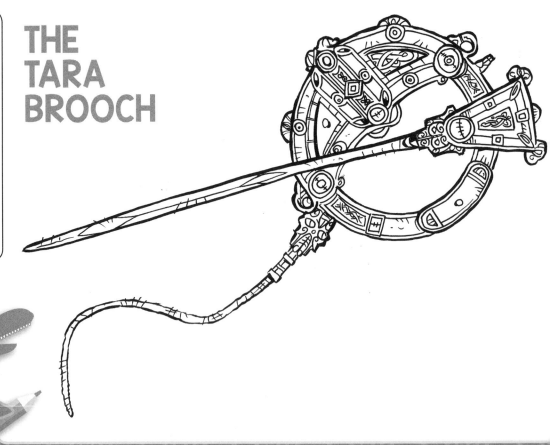

Constance Georgine Markievicz was a politician, a suffragette, a revolutionary and a countess! She took part in the 1916 Easter Rising, fighting in St. Stephen's Green in Dublin, and was the first woman to be elected to the British House of Commons.

COUNTESS MARKIEVICZ

The Giant's Causeway, in County Antrim, was caused by an ancient volcanic eruption. The volcano's cooling lava formed an area of mostly hexagonal interlocking basalt columns.

Legend has it, though, that the causeway was really built by the mythical giant warrior Fionn Mac Cumhaill, as a way to fight the Scottish giant Benandonner. Today the Giant's Causeway is one of the natural wonders of the world and is visited by almost one million people every year.

County Antrim

MORE BOOKS FROM ALAN NOLAN

FINTAN'S FIFTEEN

The worst U12s hurling team in Ireland want you! Join Fintan, Rusty, Katie and team mascot Ollie the Dog as they recruit new players, learn new skills and try to thwart the efforts of a rival manager to steal the peculiarly precious Lonergan Cup!

www.OBrien.ie

Let's Colour Ireland!

First published 2018 by
The O'Brien Press Ltd,
12 Terenure Road East,
Rathgar, Dublin 6,
D06 HD27, Ireland
Tel: +353 1 492 3333;
Fax: +353 1 429 2777

Email: books@obrien.ie
Website: www.obrien.ie
The O'Brien Press is a member of Publishing Ireland.

ISBN: 978-1-78849-005-4

Copyright for text, illustrations and layout design © Alan Nolan 2018
Editing: The O'Brien Press Limited

Published in
DUBLIN UNESCO
City of Literature

8 7 6 5 4 3 2 1
21 20 19 18

Printed and bound by Gutenberg Press, Malta
The paper in this book is produced using pulp from managed forests.

CONOR'S CAVEMAN
THE AMAZING ADVENTURES OF OGG

When best pals Conor and Charlie accidentally uncover a prehistoric man frozen in a block of ice, life suddenly gets a bit TOO interesting!

Pre-hysterical fun from Alan Nolan.

www.OBrien.ie

SAM HANNIGAN'S WOOF WEEK

It's all going to the dogs!

Animal lover and champion Irish dancer Samantha Hannigan is having a truly woof week.

She and her best pal Ajay were messing around with the amazing Brain Swap 3000 and now Sam is stuck inside the body of Barker, her neighbour's dog!

The BARKING CRAZY new novel from Alan Nolan

These books and more are available from all good book sellers or direct from **www.OBrien.ie**

Colour this picture too!